Deconstructing
INFATUATION

Merce Cardus

Merce Cardus
Deconstructing INFATUATION

This book is a work of fiction. Names, characters, places, and incidents are either products of the author's imagination or are used fictitiously. Any resemblance to actual events or locals or persons, living or dead, is entirely coincidental.

Copyright © 2011 by Merce Cardus
All rights reserved, including the right of reproduction in whole or in part in any form without written permission from the author.

ISBN-13: 978-1477481486
ISBN-10: 1477481486

Cover design by Merce Cardus

Author Photograph copyright © 2012 by Monica Galera

First Edition: June 2012

Manufactured in the United States of America

For information: www.mercecardus.blogspot.com
www.amazon.com/author/mercecardus

Also by Merce Cardus:
I say Who, What, and Where!

To my sister and livelong friend, Cinta Cardus,

with Love.

DECONSTRUCTION

Is NOT a method and cannot be transformed into one. It is NOT a critique in the Kantian sense. It is NOT an analysis in the traditional sense. It involves a certain attention to structures and tries to understand how an ensemble was constituted.

—JACQUES DERRIDA, French philosopher, Founder of "Deconstruction."

INFATUATION

Almost can equate to lust. It is NOT love, not being in-love; however, both usually start off as an infatuation. Infatuation is only an attraction for another person based only on what you initially see and not what you know about them. You do NOT know that person yet. It is only an attraction to someone based on what you WANT them to be versus who they really are.

—URBAN DICTIONARY.

CONTENTS

Sexual Tension-Kindness
Sexual Tension
1
Kindness
19

Hunger-Merging
Hunger
53
Merging
85

Infatuation-Separation
Separation
97
Deconstructing Infatuation
125

Acknowledgments
129

About the author
131

Deconstructing

INFATUATION

SEXUAL TENSION-KINDNESS
(Invisible-Intelligible)

SEXUAL TENSION

1.

HELEN opened the window to air the living room, for that Sunday they expected a crowd to come in and out. She eyed her watch and rushed out to the convenience store, while her roommate Marleen tried to jam her toilet kit into the suitcase.

At the store, Helen glanced at the magazine covers, paid for her black coffee, abruptly stopped the chitchat the salesclerk had struck up, and went straight back home. She didn't want to miss even one candidate. It was not the first time they agreed to sublet one of the two rooms, and they had never had

Deconstructing INFATUATION

any complaints, except once. It so happened that a mousy young girl had sublet Marleen's bedroom for two months. One day during her last week, she was caught poking her nose into Helen's closet and had the insolence to deny it just minutes later. Although they kept living together until the sublet was up, they shunned each other all the time. Since then, they both had to give their approval of the sublesee. It was an unbreakable rule.

By twelve thirty, the brief advertisement on Craigslist had drawn a bunch of potential roommates, though the open house was set up until 4 P.M. At six minutes of four, the doorbell rang.

"Is the sublet still available? This is Tiziano Conti," he said, offering his right hand between the door's opening.

"I'm sorry, the open house is over," Helen said, closing the door.

"No, no, no. It's not over. Come on in, please," Marleen said, pushing her aside while opening the door to let him in.

Tiziano gave them a forced smile while coming in.

MERCE CARDUS

"She is Helen Hayes, and I'm Marleen Walker," Marleen said.

Tiziano went to shake hands first with Marleen and then with Helen. He walked across the living room, looked around, and stopped by the open window. He bolted down a bite of sandwich he held in his left hand and picked a crumb from his lip. Tapping his fingers on the flat screen TV, he asked, "Is this working?"

Helen saw how some crumbs fell on the carpet, gave a resounding yes, and warned him, "Why don't you put your sandwich in your shoulder bag?"

"Easy! They are only crumbs." He put on a fake smile again and hid his sandwich in the little section of his bag.

"So what's bringing you here, to New York?" Marleen asked, ushering him to her room.

Helen heard from behind, "The Marathon and some business."

"I won't be here for the Marathon, so that week you might have the whole apartment to yourself," Helen said, touching the radiator with her right hand.

Turning around, Tiziano asked, "The whole

month?"

"No, I said just one week." Helen stared at him.

Tiziano and Marleen walked into Marleen's room. Helen went down on her knees, picked up the crumbs off the carpet with her fingertips, and placed them on her palm.

"So you are not bringing any furniture with you, are you?" Marleen asked.

"No, just a suitcase."

"Good. Let me alert you that animals are banned in this building."

"Am I breaking the law right now?"

Marleen laughed out loud.

When Helen heard the sound of steps emerging from the room, she sprang to her feet.

"So what do you think?" Marleen asked.

"It's fine. Bright and spacious. It works for me," he said, nodding.

"I'll move my clothes to one side of the walk-in closet to make room for yours. Any questions you want to ask?"

"The ad says the apartment has wireless Internet, right?"

MERCE CARDUS

"Yes, yes. There's wireless. I'll give you the code. And we've got a washer and dryer as well as many kitchen tools. Do you cook? We rarely cook, but we have it all," Marleen responded quickly, ushering him to the kitchen.

"Perhaps you'd like to share the apartment with a gay like you… I mean, a guy like you," Helen suggested, biting her lower lip afterward.

Tiziano suddenly stopped and turned on her. He gave her a wry look and said, "I'm sorry, but I'm quite confused. Do you want to sublet the room, or what?"

Helen declined to give an answer and went to sit down on the couch, crossing her arms and legs.

"Yes, yes. Of course." Marleen glared at Helen.

Tiziano and Marleen headed for the kitchen. Marleen stood at the kitchen doorway while he walked in to have a quick look.

"All right, I'll be waiting for an answer till eight," he said.

Tiziano went back to the living room to shake hands with Helen. She smiled with a touch of arrogance, but right away she looked down in

Deconstructing INFATUATION

embarrassment when Tiziano's hand crushed the crumbs she held in her hand. He frowned and then grinned slyly. He moved to the front door, thanked Marleen, who was already at the threshold, and left.

"Fabulous! He's exactly who we are looking for," Marleen said, clapping her hands once.

"What?! It seems to me he's an illiterate guy who watches TV 24/7. I weed him out!" Helen said, walking into her room.

Growing frantic, Marleen followed her and said, "This is just minor stuff. I think he's a good guy. He actually looks considerate and trustworthy. That's what we need for a month."

"Considerate?!"

"Yes, considerate. Besides, shaking hands with us proves that he's quite polite."

"Come on! I haven't seen any consideration on his part. Marleen, that jerk scoffed at me. And he might be a smoker."

"He said he doesn't smoke."

"What about that girl…"

"Who?"

"What's her name?" She looked through the

window.

"There were two women. One who asked us for a lower rent, and the other... well, all I can remember is those daisies..."

"Oh yes, the girl with the wreath of daisies in her hair."

"Come on! Are you serious?"

"Why not?"

"She's a dirty hippie."

"A what?!"

"She can go on placing flowers in her greasy hair; it stinks anyway." Marleen shivered and went on, "I'd rather have this good-looking guy sleeping in my bed than that dirty flower-power girl. Don't you find him attractive, huh?" Marleen nudged her.

"Mhmm... My boyfriend won't like it."

"Your boyfriend won't find it out."

"I'm not sure, Marleen."

"It's just for a month. What's the big deal?"

"I don't know. I don't feel like..."

"Please, I don't have any time left," Marleen begged her.

Helen clenched her jaw and afterward took a

Deconstructing INFATUATION

deep breath.

"Sooo?"

"Okay. Call him up!"

2.

THE next day, Helen got up early. She rushed to take a shower, applied light makeup, combed her straight brunette hair, and cleared one shelf in the bathroom. She went back to her room to get dressed in her white blouse, tight-fitting gray vest, and black suit with a skirt, all neatly pressed. She jammed two files into her extra-large handbag, put her high-heeled shoes on, grabbed her raincoat, and left the apartment, locking the door. On the train, she pulled out one file and read a manuscript without lifting her eyes for eight stops. Every once in a while, she jotted down some corrections in the margins.

Stepping inside the Literary Agency, she said good morning with a thin smile to Laura Miller, the receptionist, and headed toward her open cubicle, raising her head slightly to her colleagues on her way.

Helen checked out her in-box and sighed. An intricate morning was awaiting her. She had to push meetings forward because of two cancellations at the last minute. She hated to reschedule her well-planned agenda, especially when it was caused by recent published writers, whose initial success had gone to their head faster than champagne bubbles.

Later, back home, she noticed the front door was unlocked, and she flew into a rage. She closed the door with a bang, rested her back against it, and regained her breath. Her new roommate jerked open his bedroom door, startling her.

"The Internet is not working, and we can only watch some Latino channels on TV," he said.

"Huh?" Helen looked dazed.

"I'm saying that the Internet is not..."

"The Internet should work and the television... Why don't you go out to have fun?" she blurted, walking into her room.

"Easy! That was not the deal," he said, leaning both hands on the doorframe.

She sighed and put her extra-large handbag on her chair. "Let's start out with the Internet. My roommate gave you the code, right?" she asked and walked right past him into his room. He followed her.

"Yes, it doesn't work," he replied.

"All right, doesn't work, doesn't work... Let's see. Mhm..." She bent over his computer and checked it out. "It doesn't work, Mr. Whiner, because this combination of numbers and letters is wrong. Do you mind?" Helen asked, pointing to the chair.

"Go ahead."

She pulled the chair out and sat down, grabbed the mouse, clicked the username 5A, and checked out the code. She deleted some letters while his strong-looking hands, which rested on the desk, distracted her for a split second.

"And these are capital letters. See?"

"Okay."

"All right. I'm tired. Good night," she said, getting up.

Helen headed to her room when he stood in front of her, blocking her way.

"Excuse me," she said, lifting her eyebrows.

"TV?" he asked.

"Sorry, we don't pay for cable."

"Why?"

"What for? Nobody watches TV in this apartment."

He stared at her for a few seconds and got out of her way.

She walked out and, without looking back, said, "By the way, always lock the front door when you come in!" Helen shut her bedroom door with a bang.

3.

HELEN started her Tuesday morning at the Literary Agency by writing down a list of roommate "do's and don'ts."

She was a bit concerned about sharing space with the opposite gender, since she had heard many horror stories, though she suspected some of them must have been sheer urban legend. In her late thirties, surprisingly, she had never lived with a man. Since Mark and she began dating three years ago, they had lived not only in different apartments but also in different neighborhoods. Neither of them had ever brought up the subject. She wondered if the distance between them kept them from falling into a routine. The silence between them was quite telling. So she thought clearing things up with Tiziano was the best way to not fall into absurd discussions later.

Rule number one: don't leave food in the bedroom.
Rule number two: don't have overnight guests.
Rule number three: the front door must always be locked behind you coming in as well as out.
Rule number four: keep the bathroom door open when it's not occupied.

That morning the bathroom was so steamy, she felt she had had a Turkish bath which had transported her to an Eastern Hamman for a while. When she went back to her list, she wrote down:

Rule number five: the windows must be opened when you cook.
Rule number six: definitely the dirty dishes must be washed up after cooking (or eating).

MERCE CARDUS

After writing down the word "eating," she looked at her ticking watch. She always went out to lunch right at noon, so even though her stomach was already screaming, she ignored it and decided to wait. She continued with her list.

Rule number seven: Garbage guide.

First, the blue can is for recyclables: Only containers that have a triangle on the bottom get rinsed out and thrown in this can.

Second, there is a food garbage bag in the fridge. Anything that has food wrapped in it—plastic or paper—or leftover take-out goes to this bag.

Third, paper: it goes in the trash room or leave it on top of the blue can, and I'll throw it out.

And fourth, the brown can is for everything else.

Then, Helen pondered for a while where the list should be placed in the apartment. She mentally crossed the threshold, looked at the nude walls, followed by the two bedroom doors, one in front of the other, walked through the living room, going all the way around, and stopped in the kitchen. She would stick the list on the fridge. It was the most usual place for lists. She folded the list and slipped it into her extra-large handbag. She had a look at her watch again.

It was noon. She went out for lunch.

KINDNESS

4.

A launch meeting had detained her longer than expected, and although it was Friday late afternoon, Helen returned to the Literary Agency to read the queries her assistant, Karen Smith, had left on her neat desk.

She had been in this business for ten years, but still was stunned by how many aspiring authors tried to get published by writing elaborate compelling query letters and sending them out to the agencies without rest. She herself had completed a children's book right when she got her Ph.D. in Classical

Deconstructing INFATUATION

Literature. It never saw the ligth of day. Many times she wondered if she lacked the tenacity that flowed through the veins of would-be authors, since she certainly knew the odds of getting the attention of a publisher were extremely low. Perhaps she didn't have the guts to keep writing when nobody might ever read what she bloodily put down on paper. Her sensitivity to rejection soon found an anesthetic shelter; she became a guide dog for these Trojans of literary achievement. For that Friday, she had set out to review ten queries, plus the attached first three chapters of every manuscript. By dusk, the answering machine's auto-answer light was on.

The first line of the last query e-mail made her chuckle, so she went on reading until she got distracted by her cell phone vibrating. She assumed it was Mark calling her from out of town. She thought for a second of telling him about her recent roommate, her male roommate. She grabbed her cell phone, checked the ID, and sighed. It was Emily Jung. Over the phone, Helen convinced her close friend to pick up some take-out pizza and Peronis for dinner. More than eating some pizza, her friend was eager to meet the charismatic, confident, and quite good-looking roommate, the Alpha male, as Helen described him after Emily made her talk.

When she hung up, she wondered if Tiziano would be at home. She was unaware of his schedule. She didn't know if he even had friends in town. Would she feel compelled to invite him to eat pizza with Emily and herself?

The first week had whizzed by, and she hadn't established the sort of relationship she wanted to have with him: just roommates who say hello and goodbye as neighbors do, acquaintances who share small talk sometimes, or friends who care about each other. "No, the last one is certainly a ridiculous idea," she said out loud. There was no need, especially since they would be sharing a place for such a short period of time. With her roommate Marleen, they had forged a relationship somewhere between acquaintances and friends. They had seldom gone to the movies together and had never gone out with their respective friends, though they had shared lots of girl talk. After all, sharing space and time for seven years carried its own weight. Helen kept pondering over it for a few minutes. She concluded that since things had not started too well between them, and they were about to live together for virtually a month, it would be better to build a good rapport.

Emily and Helen emerged from the subway station at East 86th Street, and the drizzle made them walk three blocks up in a rush. They stopped off at the pizza place for a moment.

The lights in the living room were on. Emily plopped herself down the couch, and her head motioned toward Tiziano's bedroom. Helen touched the radiator with her right hand, giving a little scream. Then, she placed the pizza on the coffee table and went to rap on his door.

"Tiziano."

"Come on in."

She opened the door slowly, hoping he was all dressed.

"Hey, how are you?" he asked, rolling around in his chair.

"Hi, I... I mean we, my friend and I are having pizza tonight, and I... I mean we... well, do you want to join us?" Helen managed to ask him haltingly.

"I'm Italian. I can't say no to a pizza," he said, having a big smile on his face.

She plastered a smile on and, as she turned around, made a face at Emily and went to search for some napkins. Emily moved over to let Tiziano sit down.

"So, Tiziano, what city are you from?" Emily asked him.

"I'm from Florence."

"Maquiavelo, Dante, Da Vinci... " Helen recited, standing on tiptoe to reach up to the upper cupboard.

"Awesome. Dante Alighieri is my favorite classic author," he said in Helen's ear, after jumping up to help her to grab the napkins.

"Thanks," she said, taking a pile of napkins.

Helen placed three beers onto their coasters and sat down on the couch right next to Emily.

"Tiziano, so you are into books, too. Interesting..." Emily said, nodding. "Let me tell you, Helen is a bookworm. Have you happened to see the bookshelves in her bedroom?"

Helen kicked her with her foot.

She let out a gasp and said, "I mean, of course, you have not gotten into her room… ahem, yet… Well, she has books all over: in her closet, on the floor, under the bed…"

"Emily, he got it," she interrupted sharply and changed the conversation. "Do you like the pizza?"

"Yes, it's good. Spicy but good," Tiziano replied.

"Really?! I thought Italians were really picky with the pizza and pasta. Too much oil for my taste," Emily said, soaking the pizza's oil with the napkin. "So your roommate Marleen is getting married soon, right?"

"Yes, her boyfriend has been traveling back and forth to Europe for four years because of some visa issues or something, and they've just decided to stop the constant separation."

"It's remarkable how he had never been so interested in her until she accepted the proposal," Emily said.

"A visa is certainly appealing."

They howled with laughter.

"And how have they dealt with such a long-distance relationship so far?" Tiziano asked, gulping some beer down.

"Well, it looks like it runs in the family here." Helen giggled and went on, "I am in a long-distance relationship. My boyfriend seemingly lives in the same city as I do, though he is a crazed road management consultant who travels 350 days a year. Now he is most likely in a Motel 6 in Dubuque, Iowa."

"Where the hell is that?"

"Nowhere, Emily, nowhere."

"Her boyfriend is the epitome of Mr. Platinum-Gold-Diamond-Titanium Awards guy. I wish I had those benefits…" Emily sighed.

"Emily, Mr. Platinum-Gold-Diamond-Titanium Awards guy goes on a jaunt from the airport, the taxi, the hotel room, the conference room, the taxi, and back to the airport. Nothing fancy."

"I like airports. Some day I will take a flight… "

"So are you having affairs while your boyfriend is *en route*?" Tiziano asked her.

Helen almost choked. "Excuse me?!"

"Yes, I am asking you if you meet other guys…"

His cell phone rang. He put his beer on the glass table and ducked into his room to answer it.

Helen placed his beer back onto its coaster, wiped the water ring off the glass table with the back of her hand, and murmured frantically, "Emily, I am trying to be polite. You see, right? You see…"

"Calm down, Helen."

"Calm down?! Have you heard his 'Are you having affairs…?' Who the hell is he to ask such a…" she said, gesturing.

"Shhh… He's coming."

"I was saying that I am sure your boyfriend has, let's say, some friends out there, or are you so naïve to believe him pristine 350 days a year?" He chuckled and stopped abruptly.

Helen's face tensed.

He quickly added, "I don't mean to meddle in your relationship, though. My apologies, if I did."

"Okay. It's all right. Well, I don't know what he does out there, and honestly I don't want to know."

"So you both are dishonest with each other."

"Dishonest? Better not to talk about such things, Tiziano. I guess he might have had a flirtation sometime, or something. Nothing serious, just occasionally. We are realistic, for God's sake!"

Emily turned her head right and left, as if she were following the ball in a tennis match.

"And you?"

"Me? Hum… I am not going to say I have been the Virgin Mary during the whole… the whole relationship, especially at the beginning, when Mark and I started to date."

"I see."

"You know, when you start dating, you don't know if the other person goes out just with you or if he's also dating other women. I guess until you see the commitment from both sides…"

"I see."

"Well, for me it was not a commitment."

"I gotcha. If you both talked about that," Tiziano said, biting a piece of pizza.

"Talked exactly about what?"

"About the level of commitment."

"No, no, no. I've never talked about that with

him, but it was implied. Besides, they were nobody."

"They?"

"They, only two, okay?" she said, embarrassed.

He gave her a wicked look.

"But I never crossed second base with them," she put in, flustered.

"Second base?"

"Don't you know what second base is?"

He shook his head.

"Well, it's our particular second base," she said, pointing out Emily and herself.

He nodded in agreement, waiting for the explanation.

"We consider first base kissing and touching."

He smirked.

She continued, "Second base is lovemaking."

"Interesting… And third base? Is there any third base?"

"Of course, there is a third base. Third base is seeing the guy again after having slept with him."

"Hmm… Interesting." He nodded thoughtfully.

Helen grabbed another piece of pizza and took a bite, chewing frantically.

MERCE CARDUS

"If you make love with someone for a second time, there is a deep reason aside from sexual attraction," Emily remarked.

5.

ON Sunday morning, Helen went out to the convenience store around the corner. She leafed through some magazines, chatted to the salesclerk about the content of her extra-large handbag, and ended up buying the paper and a large black coffee, as usual. She thought she would prepare a cheese omelet, a bagel with raspberry jam and butter, and she would enjoy every bite reading *The New York Times* from beginning to end. She delighted in the reading, sitting on the couch in the silence of the living room all throughout the day. Helen was used to hearing Marleen get up early on weekends, carrying outfits out the door, banging the hangers on the walls on her way out. Today at dawn, she had heard the shower, but she had fallen back to sleep at once.

At home, she left the thick paper on the couch and went out to the kitchen. She pulled two eggs and the cheddar out of the fridge and scrambled them.

"Good morning. Eewh… What's this?" Tiziano asked, spitting the coffee on the floor.

She let out a gasp of astonishment.

"Sorry, if I've disturbed you."

"Hellooo, that's my coffee!" she said, snatching the carton cup out of his hands.

"That's not coffee, my dear. That's water with some powder shit. Don't you have a coffee machine?"

"I usually don't have time to drink coffee at home. But this is pretty good. It's from…"

"Let's have brunch out."

"I'm making it," she said, irked.

She placed the plate on the stove, grabbed some paper towels, and reached down to wipe the coffee stain off the floor. She threw the dirty paper away into the brown can and grabbed the plate. Tiziano took her plate from her hands and left it in the sink. She ran water into the plate right away. Then, he patted her shoulder, pushing her forward out of the kitchen. She got into her room, took her extra-large handbag and, without saying a word, they left locking the front door.

Helen was taken aback by his resolute attitude. She was virtually paralyzed. Her strong character, that always came out when she was with her boyfriend, weakened in the presence of Tiziano. As the cart is drawn by the horse, with Mark she had always been the horse. For once, she felt restful being the cart.

She had complained about Mark's sluggishness several times. If they traveled, she had to organize the itinerary and all the arrangements. If they had dinner out, she had to pick up the restaurant and make the reservation. Yet, his indifferent attitude was a negotiable one; or at least, she thought it had been so till now.

They passed by a restaurant called Barking Dog Burger, and Helen went in. Tiziano followed her.

"Boxer burger, Terrier burger, Chihuahua

Deconstructing INFATUATION

burger..." Tiziano listed the menu, astonished.

"Yes, isn't it fun?"

"Fun, eating dog?" he said, bewildered.

"Well, it's not dog... you know..."

He glanced at her above the menu and said, "Helen, bow wow... you have me as a dog, too. Want a bite of Tiziano burger?"

Helen burst out laughing.

The waitress placed down two glasses of water and told them to call her when they were ready to order.

"What if we get up and leave?" he said.

"What?! But the waitress has already brought us the water..."

Tiziano grabbed her right hand, and they went out splitting their sides as two pipsqueaks who had done a childish thing.

They ended up at an Italian restaurant on the corner. Helen grasped that Tiziano was asking for a table for two in Italian.

"So I guess you like *The Divine Comedy*?" she asked, playing with the salt shaker.

"Oh yes. *Divina Commedia*. I have read it many

times."

"Really?"

"There are so many versions and each one relates to a different world. For instance, the ancient ones focused only on teleological arguments. Then, the comments stressed the historical in the beginning of the 19th century. And nowadays we just find the aesthetic sense."

"And which is the aesthetic sense?" she asked.

"Beauty just implies truth."

"I never looked at it that way. But I think beauty is rather subjective, Tiziano. I like this chair, but you might not like it."

"This is just a sense of taste, Helen. Truth walks side by side with beauty, so to speak; yet it has nothing to do with how much truth you can stand."

She was gawking at him when the waiter came with the dishes and warned them to not touch the hot plates.

He continued, "For instance, your boyfriend is cheating on you. Can you bear that?"

"I said I'm not sure about that," Helen answered with a straight face.

Deconstructing INFATUATION

"You said you don't want to know."

"Yes, I don't want to know. Now what?"

"You are running away from the truth."

"If you say it…"

He nodded.

"But anyway I can't see where the beauty is if my boyfriend is cheating on me."

She dropped the salt shaker on the table, opening the lid and scattering some salt on the tablecloth. Helen blushed with shame, and started to pick pinches of salt and put them back into the salt shaker.

"Leave it," he said.

"What?! Why do I have to leave my boyfriend?" she asked, little miffed.

"I said leave the salt where it is."

"Mhm…" Helen looked down her plate and took a bite of the filet mignon.

"Helen, beauty stems always from truth. You can either look the other way or pursue it. It does not matter your liking. No matter if you don't like your boyfriend cheating on you, or if you like it."

"It's complicated." She looked right through

him.

"Truth is what it is, Helen," he said, wiping his mouth.

She downed her wine in one gulp, flustered.

"So Helen, have you read Dante's *Divine Comedy*?" Tiziano asked, pouring some red wine in her glass.

"Yes, I read an English version out loud a long time ago."

"Exactly! *Il canto* requires its intonation. I'm sure you will know that in that time the printing press had not already been invented, so the knowledge was passed on orally."

She smiled slightly in affirmation.

Leaving the restaurant, Tiziano and Helen heard a clap of thunder.

"I'm gonna hail a taxi," Helen said, getting closer to the road.

He stopped her by grabbing her arm and said, "A taxi? We live five blocks away."

"It's going to rain."

"I don't think so. Those thunderclouds are really far away," he said, raising his head to the sky.

Deconstructing INFATUATION

They turned around to walk through the crosswalk when a driving rain began to drench them. Tiziano sniggered at Helen's alarmed expression. She realized it and chortled.

Seeing the traffic moving toward them, they crossed the road in a rush.

"Have you ever walked in the rain?" he shouted.

She shook her head.

"There's always a first time," he said, grabbing her hand.

She shivered.

Although quivering with cold, she found it thrilling to wade through the water, even stepping into the puddles. One block away from the apartment, she smiled timidly at him and dropped his hand.

At the front door, Helen asked him to take his mudsoaked shoes off. He obeyed. She took hers off, too. He let her use the bathroom first.

Helen enjoyed herself taking a hot shower. She stepped out of the tub, and in front of the mirror she looked at herself for a moment. She leaned her head forward and touched her hair, noticing some gray hairs growing out from the beginning of her forehead, which reminded her to go to the hairdresser's soon. Afterward, her eyes studied her considerable breasts. At her age and from then on, she knew the fibrous tissue, which kept the structure of the breasts firm, was going to decrease, and hers already started to show signs of falling slightly. Plastic surgery had never crossed her mind, though. She already had a boyfriend who had never had any complaints; at least, he had not showed any concern. Suddenly, her confidence faded. Trying to regain it again, she recalled she had read somewhere that the great passions had never been moved by a perfect body but by an evolved mind. Had she ever felt passion for him?

She lifted her boobs exaggeratedly with both hands and grinned at herself again. Then, Helen tied a towel around her chest and gazed at Tiziano's shelf: two razor blades, shaving gel, a stick deodorant, talcum powder, a toothbrush, toothpaste, and a bottle of cologne, Obssession by Calvin Klein.

"Obsession," she murmured, peering into the mirror.

Deconstructing INFATUATION

She smirked at herself and went out to her bedroom.

In the corridor, she bumped into Tiziano waiting his turn for the bathroom.

"Your turn," she said.

He had a good look at Helen, and she smiled shyly. Suddenly, she sneezed all over him.

"I'm sorry," she said.

He shook his head and said, "It's nothing. You better put some clothes on."

She nodded.

He kept staring at her for a while. Then, she stepped into her room while he walked into the bathroom. As he closed the bathroom door, she called him.

"Tiziano."

He opened the door and stuck his head out.

"Yes?"

"I had fun today," she said.

"Me too."

6.

HOURS later, Tiziano was watching television while hearing Helen fussing about in her bedroom. He turned the volume up. She emerged from her room and headed for the bathroom without uttering a word. She paced back and forth while he looked at her out of the corner of his eye. She didn't stop glancing at her watch. He checked his watch, too. It was 9:33 P.M. Suddenly, her cell phone rang, and Helen shut herself in her room again. Five minutes later, she went out to the living room, all dressed up but barefoot.

Deconstructing INFATUATION

"What are you watching there?" she asked.

"He has stood you up, right?" Tiziano asked, gulping a Peroni.

She nodded and said, "He's stuck in a fuckin' airport."

"*Vaffanculo*... I'm sorry."

"It's okay... So what are you watching here?" she asked again, sitting next to him on the couch.

"Ice skating contest. It's hilarious. This guy is really good but has a big schnozzle."

"Oh yeah, it's big," Helen said, unimpressed.

"And before him, you should have seen a quite peculiar couple. She was so fat, the guy could not hold her. He made a sweaty effort to lift her up... ha, ha, ha."

"Don't be bad."

"I'm not! The grace of dancing in ice skating comes not only from the artistic but also the lightness of their movements. I want you to judge it for yourself. Let's see if they come out again."

Helen saw the water had dropped on the glass table and overlooked it. She rose and went out to the kitchen to fetch the last Peroni and some cheese-flavored snack crackers. Sitting down on the couch, she put the beer and the snacks on the glass table.

"Ha, ha, ha… Oh my goodness!" she said, giving him a pat.

"I told you so. This ice skating contest is for cracking up."

After a while, her anger had been eased by beer and laughter. She stood up and cleared the coffee table. While walking into her room, she turned around and said, "Good night, Tiziano."

"Good night, Helen."

She shut the door behind her.

7.

AT eleven-twenty the next morning, while reading a final manuscript of 332 pages, Helen received a phone call. It was Mark. He apologized to her and tried to make up by saying they had to do something really nice, yet left the planning to her. She sighed.

Two minutes later, her cell phone buzzed with a sms. She thought it was Mark but was Tiziano. She grinned.

<<Schnozzle's invasion. I saw one in the subway. Ready for a good coffee? I'm in your hood.>>

Deconstructing INFATUATION

She giggled under the surprised look of her assistant who was just coming in to her cubicle.

"Give me a minute, please," Helen said to Karen.

She nodded.

Helen answered him back quickly:

<<Okay>>
<<In ten minutes@Flatiron>>
<<Yes!>>

She hashed out her agenda with Karen, placed the manuscript in a folder, and turned her chair around to look through the window. The Flatiron Building stood majestically in front of her. How many hours had she spent staring at the stately building? Yes, she knew that beauty was an uncontrollable force. "Like truth," she added out loud. She truly admired the so-called fool who had designed the building against all predictions of failure. He was simply another hero, another Trojan. She stood up and went by the window, gazing at the mob passing by. Her mind transported her to 1903, when men used to hang out around 23rd Street to ogle the women's ankles when their long skirts were lifted by the strong winds. She grinned and woke up from her daydreaming. Then, Helen glimpsed Tiziano with his hands in his pockets and exited the Agency.

They said hello to each other. Tiziano brought her to the Italian market, *Eataly*. Amid the bedlam of the market maze, walking side by side, he managed to explain to her the source of the Italian cuisine, as well as the customary gatherings like the nightly *aperitivo* and the *Natale panettone*. His culinary descriptions—a delicious branzino with aromatic herbs, fresh pasta, and a rich tiramisu *inter alia*—seemed like those coming out of a great cook, or perhaps they were coming out of the natural wisdom that Italians acquire from their mothers. Helen was quiet, as an attentive student eager to learn the daily lesson. They stopped off at a coffee shop, and he ordered two *ristrettos*. He drank up the coffee in one gulp, and Helen followed suit.

On their way out, he took a packet of *taglietoni* from a shop stand. Tiziano explained to her in detail how to cook it with truffles, making her mouth water.

Then, he placed the packet back and grabbed another one.

"And this one, this thin spaghetti, I'm going to prepare it *alla carbonara per te, signorina.*"

She smiled shyly.

"Can you hold the spaghetti's packet for a second?"

"Yes," she said.

Tiziano gave a twenty dollar bill to the stallkeeper and waited for the change. He took the change, and they went out. At the market's door, they stood looking at each other for a while.

"Give it to me," he said.

She blushed, realizing they had never kissed, not even a childish kiss on the cheek.

"The spaghetti, Helen," he said, snatching the packet out of her hands.

"Ah!" she pronounced.

He grinned.

Then, unable to bear the awkward lull, Helen merely said bye and left.

HUNGER-MERGING
(Invisible-Intelligible)

HUNGER

8.

A smell of roasted coffee woke her up. Helen rolled out of bed, put her robe on, and headed for the kitchen, rubbing the sleep from her eyes, doing her hair with her hands, and pulling the sleeve down slightly and thus leaving her right shoulder bare. Tiziano had bought a brand-new espresso maker with Brazilian-coffee capsules, and he, wearing sport clothes, was making some toast.

"Too much smoke, Tiziano, beware of the fire alarm. Rule number five," she admonished him, pointing out the roommate "do's and don'ts" list hanging on the fridge.

"Easy!"

The fire alarm went off.

"I told you so! Open the windows, please!"

"Easy, Helen, easy! Breathe! One, two, three; one, two, three…" he shouted with his arms open.

Helen convulsed with laughter. His easy way of life amazed her. He got rid of the burned toast, and she placed them into the trash bag in the fridge. He made more, also putting a bagel on the broiler station for her. That morning she forgot about always being punctual at work. They had breakfast, leaning against the marble kitchen counter.

"Which part of *The Divine Comedy* do you like the most, Tiziano?" she asked.

"The fifth Canto."

"The Hell, huh?"

"*L'inferno* depicts the truth."

"I suspected you'd tell me something of the sort," she said sarcastically nodding.

He grinned and biting his toast said, "Helen, life was not given to us for living cautiously."

"Ah not?"

He shook his head.

"What's the purpose, then? To find the truth?" she said, grinning from ear to ear.

"To find yourself," he managed to answer with a mouthful.

She nodded and said, "It makes sense since the Divine Comedy tells of Dante's inner journey."

"Yes, it's an inner journey."

"Well, I try to take control over my life."

"I'm not talking about that but totally the contrary. We don't have to control life but learn to flow in the river of life. Life was given to us as a perfect chance to awaken and transcend."

"This is a religious approach. Let me remind you that although Dante accepted the world's evil, he believed he had to adore a non-understandable God. That means God is in control, after all."

"It's a spiritual one," he said, shaking the crumbs off his hands. "And yes, God is in control if, and only if, you don't want to be responsible for your life."

"And what's the trigger to awaken?"

"I might say the trigger is danger."

Deconstructing INFATUATION

"Danger?"

"For instance, let's take my favorite Canto placed in Hell, Circle two. Francesca da Rimini and her husband's brother, Paolo Malatesta, committed adultery, and they were murdered by her husband, Gianciotto. Although exploring the fine line between love as a power of attraction toward the beauty of a person and lust as a possessive sexual desire, Dante confined them to hell forever, since not only did they let their appetites sway their reason, but also they were unrepentant, trying to justify their sin. Dante did not have interest in the sin per se. He accepted it as truth has to be accepted. Even, I would say, he didn't care a rap the way their lust was brought to light. The trigger, the danger, began when it was occuring as something more intimate and magical: how Francesca and Paolo realized they were in love, when it came to the time of sweet sighs. He focused only on two people who tell each other that they are in love but were not aware of it."

Helen gave him a frightened look, took a glance at her watch, and said, "We should leave that conversation for later. I gotta run. I'm late."

MERCE CARDUS

She rushed into her room, got dressed in the wrinkled clothes left yesterday on the arm rest, and stopped by the bathroom to apply light makeup, floss her teeth, and comb her hair. She placed her high-heeled shoes into the extra-large handbag, put her sneakers on, and went out running and pushing commuters and gawking tourists all along her way.

She waltzed into the Agency, and Laura Miller, who was on the phone, said "Hold on," and asked Helen if she was sick or had a little mishap. Helen said everything was all right and didn't give any further explanation, even though Laura was waiting for one.

She spent her day wondering who Tiziano was. Helen's mind harbored manifold questions. What did he like, aside from Dante's *Divine Comedy*? What did he do for a living? What was his life in Florence like? What kind of business was holding him in town? What did he think of her? What was the truth that lay behind their encounter?

She thought for a while if he disappeared without notice and she went looking for him, like in one of those detective films, she only would be able

Deconstructing INFATUATION

to describe him as a mid-fortyish guy, with a mane of dark hair, whose smile enlightened the space where he was, even when he was sniggering at her. He had slightly slumped shoulders, though his sturdy body gave her steady signs of his routine workout. She knew that he would be running the twenty-six miles and 385 yards in two weeks, and even though she felt like cheering him on at some point during the race, by then she would be out of town with Mark. Had she forgotten that she had a boyfriend?

Her daydream was stopped by a knock on her cubicle wall.

9.

THE next morning, she was late to work again. She had never enjoyed breakfast as much as she did with Tiziano. Although they talked about the chilly weather and about why bagels had holes in them, it was *il Sommo Poeta* that drew them to an endless chatting. With Mark, on the other hand, the conversations had been always confined to analysis of business problems and description of hotels and landmarks of cities he happened to have seen through the taxi windows.

When she realized the time, she rushed into her

room, got dressed in the wrinkled clothes left yesterday on the arm rest again, and stopped by the bathroom to apply light makeup, floss her teeth, and comb her hair. She placed her high-heeled shoes into the extra-large handbag, put her sneakers on, and went out running and pushing commuters and gawking tourists all along her way.

That morning, as Helen was entering the Agency, her boss stood beside the receptionist, looking at her with disapproval. Now she would have to be the last one to leave the agency. She grumbled. She would miss watching ice skating contest with Tiziano. Last night, he had promised her they would go skating at Bryant Park. Helen took phone calls from clients, proofread some pages of a manuscript, held some staff meetings, but she never left her cell phone unattended, checking it every five minutes. She didn't want to miss any message, any phone call from him.

Helen felt the day drag. At nine, she was very tired and eager to get home. In her neighborhood, she stopped by the convenience store to grab some take-out food.

MERCE CARDUS

The living room was silent. When she crossed the threshold, her smile faded. She stood in the kitchen and ate her pre-made meal. She thought she should call up Mark but didn't. Last week he had been in Ohio; this week he was in Minnesota. It was hard to understand what he liked about that job. It was late, and she didn't feel like having a chat. She just wanted to crawl into bed. The smell of Patchouli-scented cologne made her breathe deeply. Tiziano was at home. She had a look at his door and went into her room. She got undressed, threw her clothes into the hamper, put her pajamas on, and lay down in bed under the covers.

The apartment was still until she shouted.

"Oh my God, oh my God, something bit me, something bit me!!!"

Right away Tiziano knocked on her door, asking, "Are you okay? Can I come in?"

"Come on in! I have bed bugs!!!" Helen shouted desperately, jumping up and bouncing on the bed.

"Easy, Helen, easy. You're going to fall down. Please, get down, for God's sake!"

"There are bed bugs in my bed!"

Deconstructing INFATUATION

"Easy!"

"I don't want to sleep here. There are bed bugs, Tiziano!"

"You already said that. Let me find them," he said, holding her hands.

"Look at this?" She showed him her red chest.

"Okay, sit down... I'm going to find them."

While he started to undo the bed, Helen stood up to take the other end of the sheet, and they both aired it.

"*Allora*, one big bed bug!" Tiziano hollered, holding up a book that had gotten tangled in her sheets.

She snatched Dante's *Divine Comedy* out of his hands, threw herself on the bed, and rolled around laughing. He broke up, lying down too.

"Going over the Cantos?"

"I'm catching up," she said sheepishly.

"I see." He gave her an impish smirk.

They looked into each other's eyes.

"The sweet sighs began after reading the adulterous story of Sir Lancelot and Queen Guinevere," she said, lighting up.

"Right on."

"Queen Guinevere, wife of King Arthur, kissed Lancelot, the most valiant of Arthur's knights of the Round Table. On the contrary, Francesca gave the romantic initiative to Paolo."

They kept gazing intently into each other eyes.

"The repentant was banned in hell. Francesca knew she had sinned, but even so she made her choice: to keep loving Paolo," Tiziano said.

Helen flinched slightly.

"Oh, this is smooth!" Tiziano remarked, stroking the blanket with his face and hands.

Helen dissolved into stitches.

"There's nothing, Helen," he assured her.

They exchanged an intense glance within inches of each other. After the deep silence, Tiziano said, "You'd better take off your nightgown."

"Huh?"

"I guess the bed bug is stuck on your nightgown."

Helen nodded. She went out to the bathroom, carrying her robe while scratching her chest. She closed the bathroom door behind her and took a deep breath.

Helen shed her nightgown quickly. She looked at her chest in the mirror and kept scratching. She opened the medicine cabinet and found an ointment. She rubbed it on her chest and grimaced as it stung. She put her robe on. When she returned to her room, he snatched her nightie out of her hands and aired it. A rust-colored insect fell off on to the bed.

"You see, you see…" she said, grinning from ear to ear.

"Yes, just one."

"Thanks, Tiziano. Much appreciate it."

"You're welcome. Let's go to bed now." He winked and left closing her door behind him.

10.

ON Thursday and Friday, Helen hadn't crossed Tiziano's path. She had had breakfast slowly hoping to meet him in the kitchen, but his toast had never made it out of the fridge. She had watched the ice skating contest while checking out her mail, but the living room had not been touched by his Patchouli-scented cologne.

She went to the movies with Mark on Saturday and spent the night in his 35-floor apartment on Wall Street. She didn't like his cold Bachelor's-type apartment, but at his hideaway they were able to stay together alone. She made love with Mark while random thoughts of Tiziano crossed her mind, followed by her wondering how making love with Tiziano would be. She imagined him as a passionate lover, and that created a wild desire, turning her on. An image of Kim Basinger swinging her hips behind the roller blind appeared in her head. She came.

In the morning, she jumped out of bed and took a quick shower, thinking how Mark and she had fallen into such a routine lovemaking. Afterward, she stepped out of the tub and dried herself off with a towel. She shouted to him from the bathroom that she had to rush to her place because she was very behind on her reading.

When Helen crossed the threshold of her apartment, Tiziano rushed toward her with an unfamiliar apron in his hands and tied it around her. "*Signorina, oggi, come primo, abbiamo spaghetti alla carbonara.*"

She looked amused and said, "I guess there is something going on with spaghetti."

"Right on. We are going to make spaghetti."

"Tiziano, I'm not a good cook."

"I'll teach you," he said, grabbing her shoulders with his hands.

He put the water on to boil and took three eggs, butter, powder cheese, and *pancetta* from the fridge. Helen opened the windows and sat down the stool, observing his provisions.

He looked around and said, "No, no, no. Come here."

He put her in front of him, grabbed her hands and an egg, and together they broke the egg, separating the yolk from the white. The white just squeezed from their fingers, falling into the bowl, giving her goose bumps. They did the same with the rest.

The water boiled, so he wrung out the spaghetti in his hands, as if it were a wet towel, and threw it into the water. She tacked on the rest of ingredients into the bowl, as Tiziano had showed her how to do.

"It says 8 minutes boiling, Tiziano," she said.

"Are you insulting me?" he said, defiant.

Bewildered, she looked at him.

"Italians don't count the minutes. We know when the pasta is cooked by throwing a strand of spaguetti on the ceiling. When it sticks, it's done."

She gave him a little smile.

Tiziano tried to stick one spaghetti to the ceiling as proof of his skill. It fell down. She followed suit, and the spaghetti fell on Helen's face. She laughed out loud. She found it amusing and did it several times. They all fell down. Later, she praised the dish by running a crust of bread around her empty plate. He, however, said that the dish would be better if they were in Florence because both the water and the ingredients would be different.

Helen spent the afternoon talking to Emily about Tiziano. They walked into the Diesel store, and she said Tiziano wore those types of T-shirts. Emily looked at a watch in a store window display on Prince and West Broadway, and Helen remarked that one of his watches was that brand. They ended up having a beer in Epistrophe, and she complained to the waiter, wearing huge black spectacles, about them running out of Peronis.

When Helen came back home, Tiziano was browsing a Victoria's Secret's catalog that she had left on the coffee table, along with some mail. She said hello, left her extra-large handbag on one side of the couch, and sat down next to him, their shoulders touching. He was turning the pages while picking his favorite underwear outfits.

"I like hip-huggers for women. They are sexy!" he said.

"And comfy!"

He gave her a conspiratorial wink and said, "Can I ask you a personal question?"

She nodded.

"Why don't you live with your boyfriend?"

She smiled coyly.

"You can tell me the truth." He winked.

"If I don't expect anyone to come home, I don't feel the loneliness. The loneliness starts to appear, it actually begins to hit hard when we are expecting someone and not knowing if he's going to come."

"I understand," he said, turning a page. "Fear to step forward, huh?"

"Probably."

"Fear to get vulnerable?"

"Mhmm... Yes, I guess."

"Do you love him?"

Deconstructing INFATUATION

She leaned back and bent her knees on the couch. "Tiziano, do you think one can have true feelings for two people at the same time?"

"Yes, I do."

She clenched her jaw and nodded.

"Although I also think you choose someone with whom you want to share your life."

They looked into each other eyes, and she asked, "Do you like this outfit?"

"It depends on who's wearing it," he replied, giving her a wicked smile.

She grinned from ear to ear.

"To love is to risk."

She swallowed hard and said, "And if you had already chosen, and someone else appears in your life out of the blue? I mean, do you think someone else can appear in one's life if your heart is already occupied?"

He grabbed her arm and let it fall. "If it were made of stone, it wouldn't move at all. Love is irrational. Not logical."

She nodded.

"Sometimes, Helen, whether you're single or

with a significant one, somebody appears in your life unexpectedly. We feel the need to know who this person is, the need to know exactly who this person is. Call it human force, call it solar forces, yet they have brought you this person in front of your nose. It depends on your level of awareness to see the significance of the encounter. I mean if one of them is not conscious enough, he could let her slip away. Also it could happen that they both are not aware and depart from each other."

"That's sad."

"Yes, it is. Albeit if you are destined to experience something with that person, most likely fate will bring both of you together again and again till both of you become aware of the connection."

"You mean they are destined to be together and that's why the solar forces brought them together once and again?"

"Not necessarily. Perhaps they have just to experience, or to learn, or even to realize something in themselves."

She looked fondly into his eyes.

"Once being aware of the connection, if they

both want to create a deep bond, they will have to pass beyond the veil of the physical."

"How?"

"Through a sacrifice."

"A sacrifice?" she asked, smiling.

"To love is to risk, Helen. The sacrifice is to open up, to give ourselves to the encounter freely."

She gave him a frightened look.

"If you are not ready, most likely you will renounce the deep bond with the other, keeping just an external bond."

"Do you think unfaithfulness has to be tolerated, then?"

"The unfaithfuls should be killed off and confined to hell forever, as Gianciotto did with Francesca and Paolo."

They laughed uproariously.

"It depends," he said.

"On what?"

"Are you talking about sex or a real encounter? How much truth the couple tolerates?"

"The truth, again…" she said, shaking her head.

"Helen, what would you say if your boyfriend

told you he had a beautiful encounter with a woman. Listen, I'm not talking about him being a philanderer."

"I don't know."

"Imagine that although he had that beautiful encounter, he chose to share his life with you. He made his decision. Would your love be so powerful as to stand the truth?"

"I don't know," she said, her head spinning.

He nodded and kept leafing through the catalog. "In Italy there's a famous brand called LaPerla. It's elegant and sexy." He turned his head toward her and said, "Like you."

She blushed.

11.

THE next night, Helen was already in bed when she heard the sound of the front door opening and then the lock. She leaned forward off the pillow and waited for the sound of the television. The apartment remained silent. She rolled out of bed and put her robe on. She went out to the dim living room. Tiziano was lounging on the couch. With the outside lights, she could glimpse his very crestfallen appearance. He made some room for her to lie down next to him, and she draped her legs over the arm of the couch.

Deconstructing INFATUATION

"Don't you feel well, Tiziano?" she whispered.
"I'm feeling lousy today."
"I can see it on your face. Business problems?"
"Let's say something of the sort."
"Wanna talk about it?"
He shook his head.
"Mhmm…"

Helen felt scared by his gaze and averted her eyes for a while but couldn't resist gazing back. He saw how she sighed deeply and gave a nervous giggle. She saw how he swallowed hard. His hand touched and stroked her face for a while.

"Helen," he said, gazing fondly at her.

Many emotions bubbled up on Helen's face. Tiziano's head came up to hers very slowly until his lips touched hers, pressing for a long minute. Then, he pulled back. She burst out laughing. When she stopped laughing, she pounced on him, grabbing his head with both hands. They kept holding tight to each other and kissed deeply while their tongues continuously played in and out. When she sated her hunger, she ran away to her room.

12.

IN the morning, Helen woke up an hour earlier than she did regularly and crept out of the apartment without having breakfast, not even a cup of coffee. At the Literary Agency, she called up Emily.

"What should I do Emily? Oh my goodness, we live in the same apartment."

"Yeah, this is a problem. If you quarrelled with Mark, you would go to your place, leaving some space between you. But you can't get rid of the corpse. It's in your apartment!"

"Emily!"

Deconstructing INFATUATION

"Calm down! It's a figure of speech. How come are you dating a guy while living with him, huh? You and your Platinum-Gold-Diamond-Titanium boyfriend live in different apartments, and you are dating your roommate."

"I'm not dating him. We just kissed. He kissed me so tenderly and passionately at the same time, Emily. "

"This is just the first base, darling. Now go for the second!"

"Emily, that's frickin' serious. I'm in trouble."

"So are you falling for him?"

"I think so."

"Oh boy, kick him out of your place. Now!"

"I can't kick him out. Are you crazy?"

"You don't know much about him."

"I know enough. He's handsome, wise, well-read, funny, easygoing, charming… and he's putting my life upside down!"

"Oh my! You're going to lose your Mr. Platinum-Gold-Diamond-Titanium guy. You should get rid of Tiziano as soon as possible. I think it's the best option."

"The best option?"

"Too bad you will have to return part of the rent to him."

"Emily, listen, I desire him. I desire him madly."

"Oh my, you're already in trouble. Your biochemical responses are releasing epinephrine."

"Epine-what?!"

"Epinephrine, the chemical that makes us turned on."

"I don't know what the hell that is, but when I am with him, I swear Emily, I feel fire inside. Fire!"

"Be careful, sweetie. You already know how the saying goes: he who plays with fire..."

"Stendhal was right, it's one thing to read about passion..."

"Exactly, Helen, exactly! That's the example I had on the tip of my tongue. Do you remember that I accompanied you to the Stendhal workshop thing? Whatever. You are in the crystallization journey," Emily interrupted her.

"No, no, and no."

"Yes, yes, and yes. You're admiring him and acknowledging his interest in you. You're envisioning getting his love. And most likely you are overrating him."

"I'm not projecting him as being someone perfect. I mean I am not exaggerating his magnificent qualities. You can tell that. You have met him, Emily."

"Oh yeah! I know him very well. Helen, I met him just once and he was teasing you! Remember that? Have you asked to yourself what you want from him?"

"I want him!"

"Him, him… how?"

"I can't tell now. I have a knot in my stomach. I'm confused."

"It's quite understandable since you don't know much about him."

"Well, I like 'what I already know about him' very much. Are you happier with that?"

"Did he tell you what he feels for you?"

"No, we just kissed. But it's obvious."

"Okay, what if he doesn't return the ball?"

"Well, it looks like he is willing to return the ball."

"To me, it seems as if he were willing to return the ball in the physical game. But is he willing to keep playing afterward?"

"Emily, I don't know how the game will evolve. It's something I will find out if I start the game and keep playing it. At the end, to love is to risk."

"Whoa, whoa, whoa… To love is to risk?! Coming from someone who controls everything, that statement is quite weak. The question is, is it worth it?"

"Emily, living that passion is worth half of life."

MERGING

13.

THE author Helen represented was launching her book at the Plaza Hotel. That evening she knew she would be suffering the slowness of time. She plastered on smiles and glanced at her watch constantly. Her mission as a guide dog was pretty easy. She had to talk to everybody, introducing the author to the publishers, be charming, and hand out some business cards in order to build relationships with publishers and editors, yet she didn't feel like it at all. Helen's mind solely wanted to replay scenes of her time spent with Tiziano.

Deconstructing INFATUATION

The Plaza's lobby was packed to the brim. Helen had personally invited the crème de la crème of the publishing industry. Regarding the decoration, the Literary Agency had hired Robert, a consultant with exquisite taste, who was the most coveted event designer.

"Darling, do you like the stand of the books placed under that fabulous chandelier?" Robert asked.

"Yes, it gives them lots of light."

"Fabulous, wonderful, amazing. Thank God, you like it. I know the stubborn author wanted to sit over there, but she is not the celebrity tonight," Robert said.

"Ah no?"

He shook his head.

"Who is it, then?"

"THE BOOK!" he said, shaking his head again.

"Yes, I guess… but who came first the hen or the egg, the author or the book?"

"Oh my God! Not tonight, darling. I can't stand riddles," Robert said, shaking his head again while heading for the book stand.

MERCE CARDUS

There was a jazz band, playing Sinatra's *I've got a crush on you*, right in front of the bar. Helen downed her flute of champagne and grabbed another one off a waiter's tray to replace it. Her head bopped to the song, thinking that Emily would find the whole thing sappy. Rather, she found it all romantic but nostalgic. Nostalgia was served that night as a taste of the perfect setting—music, champagne—without the man that she had installed in her apartment and into her mind.

The launch party had been a success, so a small group went up to continue the party at a penthouse overlooking the Hudson. She pretended to be indisposed and left the Plaza, losing a stiletto on her way out. She grabbed it and got into a taxi. The Pakistani cabdriver wanted to chat, but she merely said yes and no.

She ran barefoot up the five floors in no time and got in. The lights were off. She regained her breath and put her ear on Tiziano's bedroom door.

Silence.

She went to her room, threw her shoes on the floor, and turned around to go back to his door. She shook her fist at the door but right away pulled it back and returned to her room. She looked around and breathed deeply. She went back to Tiziano's bedroom door and gave it a thunderous knock.

Silence.

Suddenly, he jerked open the front door. They looked at each other for a few seconds.

"I never had the least notion that I could fall with so much emotion," she haltingly recited the song she had heard at the Plaza Hotel.

"Sinatra knew it, too."

They leaped on each other, her hands grabbing his head, while his hands ran all over her body, and their tongues continuously played in and out.

Then, he pulled back, looked fondly into her eyes and, holding her head with both hands, kissed her deeply. He grabbed her hands forcefully and faced her toward the wall. She was breathless from the change of rhythm. He traced her curves with his hands. She thought of swinging her hips like Kim Basinger in *9½ Weeks*, but the very idea made her laugh hard. He let her giggle for a while. Then, he touched her ankles with his hands, running them slowly up to her thighs. She turned around, and he sucked up her neck. She cried out and giggled.

Tiziano raised his arms. She took his sweater off. Embracing her from behind, he slowly unzipped her dress. He placed his right hand inside of her bra and his left one inside of her panties. She moaned. She unfastened his belt and pulled down his pants, letting them fall to the floor. He kicked them away. He lifted her to his room.

Their tongues continuously played in and out, their hands caressing each other's legs, waists, backs, necks, heads until their hips met. Helen's breasts pressed against his torso, and she grabbed his firm buttocks and pressed him toward her, feeling his sex inside. Their sweaty bodies merged into one, both energies creating one. The dance of love ended with Helen pressing her hand to his, as he returned the pressure.

When sunlight filled the bedroom, Helen opened her eyes, and the feast of love went on. Tiziano kissed her good morning, pulled her right leg toward him, and grabbed her foot. He licked at every finger slowly, kissed tenderly every nook and cranny of her right leg until he arrived at her sex. His tongue surrounded it and amused itself. She cried out and moaned pressing her fist to the pillow. Then, she crossed her legs around his waist and let his penis penetrate her. Their sweaty bodies merged into one, both energies creating one. The dance of love ended with Helen pressing her hand to his, as he returned the pressure.

Helen jumped out of the bed, hurried to the corridor to grab her cell phone from the floor, where she had dropped it last night, and returned to Tiziano's bed. She had trouble getting into bed. The sheets and blanket were in disarray. She chortled. While he was kicking the bed clothes, she took a glance at his room in the light of the day and glimpsed a framed photo facing down on the desk. He embraced her. They covered themselves and cuddled for a while. Later, she called the Literary Agency while he went to prepare something for breakfast.

Over the phone, Helen pretended to cough. By the time she hung up, the fire alarm was going off. Then, her cell phone rang. It was Mark. She jumped out of bed, shouting.

"Chaos, you brought chaos into my life! I watch television, drink beer during weekdays, run away from a restaurant, skip work, walk in a downpour… and I didn't know how much I love chaos till now," she cried nude, jumping on the bed.

Soon she realized the neighbor from across her building stood by his window looking at her with a silly smile. She threw herself on the bed and answered the phone under the covers.

"Helen, I called up the Agency and they told me you were sick. Are you okay?"

"I'm fine… Well, I'll be fine," she said, closing her eyes.

"What? Helen, I can't hear you. I'm at the airport. All good?" he shouted.

"I'm saying I'll be fine," she said, raising her voice.

"All right. I'm boarding. I'll be in town very late. I'll pick you up tomorrow at 8 P.M."

Helen put on her underwear and went out to the kitchen. She saw burned bagels in the brown can. She grinned from ear to ear. She grabbed the roommate "do's and don'ts" list from the fridge, tore it up, and threw it into the full brown can.

"What do you need from me, Tiziano?" she asked, looking around.

"I need all of you," he said.

Helen's face lit up.

He lifted her on the kitchen counter and gave her a loud kiss.

They ate breakfast watching television. He grabbed his blanket, and they covered up, falling asleep on the couch. When the living room became dark, he walked into his room. She followed him.

"Can I sit here?" she asked him.

"My bed is your bed."

The next day, she would depart to Tampa with Mark.

INFATUATION-SEPARATION
(Invisible-Intelligible)

SEPARATION

14.

HELEN had been out of the city with Mark for ten days. Every morning, she would gaze at the calm waters on the beach, trying to not be shipwrecked from her inner tide. Images of her time with Tiziano and questions about his final two days were coming in waves inside her mind. She would slide from the past to the future, skipping the now. She thought the present was possible only with Tiziano. The third day, lying on the beach, she confronted her fears.

"Mark, would you tell me if you had a beautiful encounter with someone else?"

He rested his book on his chest and said, "What the hell are you talking about, Helen?"

She leaned forward. "Would you?"

"Nothing of the sort."

"What?!"

"This is nuts. Are you asking me if I'm having an affair?"

"Not affairs, real encounters."

"Real encounters? What the fuck? Wait a minute. Are you seeing someone else?"

"What?! That's ridiculous."

"If you've asked, it is because... You did, right?"

"Mark, don't freak out."

"Okay! Let's forget it," he said, going on with his reading.

"Mark."

"What's wrong now?"

"Nothing. Just wondering."

"We are on vacation. It's not the time to wonder. Just relax!"

"Why do we live separately?"

"What's wrong with you?" he said, leaning his

body forward.

"Nothing."

"What is this third degree about?"

"We don't talk about us."

"We are on the beach. I'm trying to read."

"We have no plans."

"Plans for what? We are good as we are. We like it like that, right?"

She mumbled.

The following day, while he went for the papers, Helen paced back and forth in the hotel room. Suddenly, she grabbed her suitcase from the wardrobe. She picked up all her clothes and put them into the suitcase. She moved to the bathroom and picked up her toothbrush and her makeup. She placed them at the top in the suitcase and locked it. She looked around to make sure she didn't leave anything behind. Then, she took her extra-large handbag in one hand and the suitcase in the other. As she walked toward the door, her cell phone rang. She grabbed it. She sat on the bed, crossing her legs.

"Helen, I'm at the store. You want *The New Yorker*, too?" Mark asked.

Deconstructing INFATUATION

"What?!"

"I'm asking if you want me to buy *The New Yorker* for you?"

"Mhmm... Okay."

Helen burst into tears and rushed to unpack her suitcase. First, she put all her clothes back and ran toward the bathroom. She stumbled out of the bathroom, letting out a little cry. She placed her toothbrush back and looked at herself in the mirror for a while. She washed her face twice and wiped it with a towel. She went back to sit down on the bed and assured herself the next few days would pass. If time had not stopped so far, most likely it wouldn't.

The last day of her vacation, she woke up excited at 5 A.M. Half an hour later, she had packed all her stuff. Their flight back wasn't till afternoon.

Mark found a parking slot in front of Helen's building.

"Helen, I think I'll stay over. Tomorrow I don't have to go to the office till late," Mark said unloading the suitcases.

"What?! I'm exhausted tonight."

"What are you talking about? We just came

from a relaxed vacation. You lay on the beach the whole time and didn't even ride the jet ski, and you love that." He slammed the trunk shut.

"Well, I'd like to get a good night's sleep tonight." She carried her two suitcases and headed for the entrance.

"What the hell is going on here?" he asked, stopping her with his hand.

"Nothing, just tired…" She shrugged. "Why don't we go to your place?"

"I don't want to drive right now. For once we can stay at your place. Wait a minute. Who is in your apartment?"

"Who? Nobody."

"And Marleen?"

"Ah, yes, Marleen."

"You are acting weird."

"I'm just tired."

"Then, I will cuddle you all night long," he declared, following her.

Helen walked up the stairs like a death row criminal on his way to serve his sentence. "My sin deserves a *contrappasso*. It's time to pay for it. But like

Deconstructing INFATUATION

Francesca da Rimini, I don't regret it either. I remain faithful to my sin," she thought. Her heart was beating hard. When she stepped on to the welcome mat and inserted the key, she closed her eyes and clenched her jaw.

The lights were on. Her heart missed a beat. How would she explain to Mark that she was living with a guy? How would she tell Mark that she was living with her own beautiful encounter? Could he stand the truth? What was the truth in all of this?

She opened her eyes, and the apartment remained silent. Tiziano was not there. She sighed, placing her right hand to her heart.

"Marleen left the lights on."

"Mhmm..." she murmured.

Helen pushed him to her room and shut the door.

She thought she had better keep him busy. Without unpacking, she touched his crotch and kissed him desperately, provoking a boner.

"Mmm... I thought you were tired..." he said.

"Yes, I was..." she said, making him be quiet.

Half an hour later, Helen heard a key rattle in

the lock, then the door shutting with a slight bang and the lock. Her heart started to beat quickly. Her toes were wiggling. She prayed he didn't come into her room. She assured herself he wouldn't do it; he most likely would knock on her door first. But Mark was next to her.

Ten minutes later, Mark rolled out of bed.

"Where are you going?" she shouted.

"For Christ' sake, Helen, you scared me! I'm going to pee," he said, looking at her strangely.

"Can you hold it? Come here..."

"Helen, you're acting weird again. What in the hell is the matter with you? I'm going to the bathroom, you know, I have to pee," he said, putting his underwear on.

"Are you walking through the apartment like that?"

"Yes, Marleen won't get surprised. She must be sleeping."

Helen lifted her body, hardly able to breathe. She hung her bare feet off the side of the bed, waiting for him to come back.

Three minutes and twelve seconds later, he

came back to the bedroom. They lay down next to each other. He held her tight.

"Has Marleen's boyfriend moved to this apartment? I saw his stuff on the bathroom shelf."

"Mhmm…"

"Eewh… Obsession."

"Mhmm…"

"I guess that now that she's getting married, they'll be planning to move out together."

"Mhmm…"

"That's why you asked me that whole thing about living together, right?"

"Mhmm…"

"Don't worry. I think you can find some girl to become your roommate quite soon."

"…"

"You should post an ad on Craigslist but remember to specify that your roommate must be a woman. Men are untidy, and I know you can't bear anyone of us in your shiny apartment and well-planned schedule."

"…"

"Ha! I can't imagine a man here. The poor guy!

He would run away the first night."

"…"

Her moist eyes were still wide open when after twenty minutes she heard another bang and the door lock.

She looked to her left; Mark was snoring.

15.

IN the morning, Helen rushed Mark to finish his cup of coffee and leave the apartment. She told him a lie, once more, saying she had to arrive at the Literary Agency earlier than usual. Mark was a bit wary of her mood but chalked it up to "women stuff."

Thinking that she was over the hump, Helen took a slow hot shower to relax her muscles and went out to the kitchen to prepare herself a bagel and an espresso, waiting for Tiziano. Ten minutes later, she took another espresso. When she realized it was quite late, she rushed into her room, got dressed in the first clothes she found in the closet, and fished in her suitcase for the toilet kit. She passed by the bathroom to apply light makeup, floss her teeth, and comb her hair. She placed her high-heeled shoes into the extra-large handbag, put her sneakers on, and went out running and pushing commuters and gawking tourists all along her way.

Although getting to the Literary Agency half an hour late, she decided she wouldn't stay longer than six anyway. In two days, Tiziano would be departing for Italy. Worried, she wondered how she could live her life in just two days.

At 8 P.M., she called up Emily from her apartment.

"Emily, I'm going to Italy with him. Jeez, before you can utter a word, let me tell you, I've been thinking a lot lately. I mean it. And I've decided to leave. I'm going wherever he goes. If he returns to Florence, I'll go to Florence."

"Hold on, I need to call 911."

"Emily, I'm dead serious. The language might be an issue at first, but I'm sure I can learn it quite fast. Then, my job will be to find a job… ha, ha, ha…

The Agency has a partner in France, so I could open a branch in Italy for foreign rights. I guess…"

"For God's sake, Helen."

"For God's sake, Helen, what?!"

"Are you listening to what you are saying?"

"You think this is just random thoughts, huh? They are not. I spent ten whole days pondering over it."

"Helen…"

"Helen, what?! Just say it. You think that I'm going nuts, right?"

"You just met him three weeks ago. You can't leave your whole life behind for someone you've just met."

"You don't understand it, Emily."

"And your boyfriend?"

"I already made my choice, and my choice is Tiziano."

"Oh my goodness…"

"I have been living with Tiziano for three weeks so far, and I swear there is much more truth between Tiziano and me than between Mark and me."

"Does Tiziano know about your decision?"

Deconstructing INFATUATION

"No, not yet. But I'm sure Tiziano feels the same as I do."

"Shit, Helen, you don't even know if he has a girlfriend or a wife in Italy."

The face-down framed photo in his bedroom came to Helen's mind, but she erased it at once. "Emily, I think I know him."

"You think you know him?"

"Yes, I do."

"Have you asked him who he is?"

"No."

"Have you asked him what he likes?"

"No."

"Have you started exploring the ways you can bond with him?"

"Well, this is just the beginning."

"Right on. This is the beginning, so what? There's no time left to know each other better. It was awesome, but it's time to move on."

"I can't act against my feelings."

"Do you know his values?"

"No."

"Do you know his interests?"

"..."

"You don't know if there might be an intellectual, psychological, or spiritual bond with him, and you are risking everything you've gotten. All right, then, tell me what on earth you both talked about before you left on vacation with Mark?"

"We talked about Hell."

"Oh my God, you're scaring me!"

"You know what? Let's end this conversation right here. I thought you would be happy for me, as I was when you started dating Tom."

"Helen, do you need my acceptance?"

"Of course not, but a little understanding would be helpful, Emily."

"Helen, you have a crush on him! This will pass, for sure."

"Do you know what needles me?"

"Mm... Nope."

"That you don't understand what I feel inside."

"I'm all ears."

"This has never happened to me before. For once in my life I don't want to think about it. I don't want to take control over it. I just want to feel it.

Deconstructing INFATUATION

When I am with him, it's like all four elements make me feel deliriously alive. Like when I'm holding his hand, I can walk in the rain; when he's inside me, I can feel fire burning inside; and each time he approaches me, I can inhale a peaceful breeze air that makes the earth where I stand shake."

"..."

"Emily?"

"If you go to Italy, I'll come to visit you. Happy?"

"Thank you. Just wanted to hear that. I have to hang up now. I want to get dressed with some sexy lingerie I bought in LaPerla for him."

"Helen, you are crazy, but I guess we all are once in a lifetime."

"Thank you, darling."

"Have fun!"

"You bet. Ciaooo," Helen said.

Half an hour later, Helen put on her new underwear and her robe, and she grabbed one Peroni from the kitchen. She drank it, watching an ice skating contest. There was no sign of Tiziano. She thought of sending him a text. No, she couldn't do it.

MERCE CARDUS

It would seem as if she were desperate.

And she was desperate.

The first rays of light crossing the living room's window woke her up. Flustered, she ran to Tiziano's room and knocked on his door.

Silence.

She knocked again.

Silence.

She knocked harder.

Silence.

She opened his door.

A void.

16.

EMILY gave Helen a witch's phone number. She had read an advertisement for a white witch called Amanda in a paranormal magazine, though she also warned her to be careful of such charlatans.

Although Helen told Amanda that the sublet contract expired that same day, the white witch assured her that Tiziano Conti would come back home. She advised her to undo the evil eye by grabbing a room-temperature egg and passing it around her body while saying out loud, "Whatever evil spell is on me, go right away off me" and cracking it open into a water glass. She only had to do it once, yet she bought two dozen eggs. If a single bubble came out, Amanda advised, Tiziano would get back home that same night.

She cracked one open at 7 P.M. Three bubbles.
Another one at 7:30 P.M. Three bubbles.
At 8 P.M. Five bubbles.
At 9:32 P.M. One bubble.
But at 9:36 P.M. Two bubbles.
At 10:00 P.M. Five bubbles.

Helen cried desperately. She took the rest of the eggs and threw them one-by-one at the window, splashing them all over the carpet. After the last one, she sank on her knees to the floor as the tears dripped off her nose. She went on crying until she drifted off to sleep on the carpet.

In the wee hours, Marleen came back to the apartment from L.A. She got in, dropped her two suitcases, regained her breath, and quickly placed her hand over her mouth and nose. She flicked the light on and, holding her breath, made her way into the living room.

She looked the mess and opened the window.

Then, she woke Helen up. Marleen helped her stagger to her bed. Helen was murmuring while her eyes continued shedding tears.

17.

HELEN's sunglasses covered her red, teary eyes during the entire following day. Nobody in the Literary Agency asked her a single question. She spent a great deal of time staring at the Flatiron Building, asking herself what might be happening behind any window. She concluded that the building's façade hid manifold stories. Some sweet stories, other bitter stories. Or perhaps bittersweet stories; those which, even though having an undesired end, the journey has been delightful.

She glanced at her watch, it was fifteen to

twelve. She was not hungry. She got up and went out to her boss' office. She talked to her for more than two hours. Then, she went back to her cubicle to pick up her coat and her new little handbag, and she moved to the exit.

"See you tomorrow," the receptionist said to her when she stepped out.

"Take care Laura. I'm taking some days off work."

"Vacation, again?" Laura put in, biting her lip.

Helen left without answering.

She rode inside a crowded subway. She stared absentmindedly at her faint reflection in the train's window during eight stops. She exited the subway station at 86th. She stopped at the convenience store and checked out the pasta section. She smiled slightly and walked away.

Back home, she closed the door with a bang, rested her back against the door, and regained her breath. She left her little handbag in her room and walked across the apartment, looking wistfully through every room. She mentally replayed every moment of the last month.

MERCE CARDUS

In the living room, Helen closed the window.

Deconstructing
INFATUATION

MY mother used to say, "Whoever makes you laugh hard, he will make you cry madly."

And she was right. One simply can't escape from the polarities of life: dancing from light to dark, from life to death, from oneness to separateness.

A story may offer different interpretations, even with several irreconcilable and contradictory meanings. As in Francesca da Rimini and Paolo Malatesta's story in Dante's *Divine Comedy*, this story is not about unfaithfulness either. This story is about infatuation: what burns inside of oneself when we let

Deconstructing INFATUATION

ourselves fall madly for someone. Yet, even the infatuation, if deconstructed, gives us a valuable lesson, a spark of wisdom, making the temporal experience of the invisible—sexual tension, hunger, and infatuation—more relevant, since all knowledge of what we call intelligible—kindness, merging, and separation—depends on the experience of what's invisible.

I once opened a window to let someone in, and as the breeze regenerates the atmosphere, sometimes someone appears out of nowhere who regenerates our inside. Tiziano awakened my sense of hearing as I listened to the sounds of his presence, my sense of smell as I followed the aroma of Patchouli and roasted coffee across the apartment, my sense of taste as I savored his homemade meal, my sense of touch as I caressed his skin, my sense of sight as I gazed fondly into his eyes, and my feelings during the time of our sweet sighs.

He awakened my passion.

I understand now that a Trojan of literary achievement writes out of passion, out of necessity. Deconstructing what I felt for him, breaking the pure emotions, the pure feelings into pieces, in order to find my truth, has also been out of passion, out of necessity. Even if the beauty of truth is nothing else but an illusion. A necessary illusion, though.

I once opened a window to let someone in, but later I had to close it to let him out. It's self-destructive to go after someone who decides to walk away. It's self-destructive to go after someone who decides to not pass beyond the veil of the physical. I sense that we will never go ice skating at Bryant Park, that our paths will never cross again, as the yolk and the white we once separated will never become an egg again. Here it's the same entropic situation.

He left, the fragrance never did.

Helen, 2011.

ACKNOWLEDGMENTS

I offer heartfelt thanks:

> To my parents and siblings,
> for their love and unfailing support.

> To my friend Samantha Guveli,
> for her creative listening and hours of encouragement.

> To my friend Olga Martinez,
> for her support and for being my loyal reader.

> To my friend Leslie Dileo,
> for generously taking the time to edit my manuscript
> and for her invaluable advice.

ABOUT THE AUTHOR

Merce Cardus is the author of two novels, *I say Who, What, and Where!* and *Deconstructing Infatuation*. Her novels are inspirational, thought-provoking, and witty, whose themes reflect and explore the great questions of Life, constantly searching for Truth.

Earning a Master's degree in Corporate Law, she has headed her own law firm. In 2008, after a wake-up call, she began an inner journey to realize her passion and comitted to following her heart. She's currently living her passion by working on her third novel.

To learn more, visit her at:
www.mercecardus.blogspot.com
www.amazon.com/author/mercecardus

CPSIA information can be obtained at www.ICGtesting.com
Printed in the USA
BVOW010955170613

323508BV00016B/355/P

9 781477 481486